SAGINAW CHIPPEWA ACADEM
LIBRARY MEDIA CENTER
MT. PLEASANT, MI 48858

WITHDRAWN

ABOUT THE BANK STREET READY-TO-READ SERIES

More than seventy-five years of educational research, innovative teaching, and quality publishing have earned The Bank Street College of Education its reputation as America's most trusted name in early childhood education.

Because no two children are exactly alike in their development, the Bank Street Ready-to-Read series is written on three levels to accommodate the individual stages of reading readiness of children ages three through eight.

● *Level 1:* GETTING READY TO READ (Pre-K–Grade 1)
Level 1 books are perfect for reading aloud with children who are getting ready to read or just starting to read words or phrases. These books feature large type, repetition, and simple sentences.

● *Level 2:* READING TOGETHER (Grades 1–3)
These books have slightly smaller type and longer sentences. They are ideal for children beginning to read by themselves who may need help.

○ *Level 3:* I CAN READ IT MYSELF (Grades 2–3)
These stories are just right for children who can read independently. They offer more complex and challenging stories and sentences.

All three levels of The Bank Street Ready-to-Read books make it easy to select the books most appropriate for your child's development and enable him or her to grow with the series step by step. The levels purposely overlap to reinforce skills and further encourage reading.

We feel that making reading fun is the single most important thing anyone can do to help children become good readers. We hope you will become part of Bank Street's long tradition of learning through sharing.

The Bank Street College
of Education

For my mother, Winifred Vanderwerp,
with love and admiration — M. M.

Please visit our web site at: **www.garethstevens.com**
For a free color catalog describing Gareth Stevens' list of high-quality books and
multimedia programs, call 1-800-542-2595 (USA) or 1-800-461-9120 (Canada).
Gareth Stevens Publishing's Fax: (414) 332-3567.

Library of Congress Cataloging-in-Publication Data

Macdonald, Maryann.
    Hedgehog bakes a cake / by Maryann Macdonald; illustrated by Lynn Munsinger.
       p. cm. -- (Bank Street ready-to-read)
    Summary: As Hedgehog starts to make a cake, his friends stop by, one by one, and
each has advice for the project.
    ISBN 0-8368-1619-6 (lib. bdg.)
    [1. Cake--Fiction. 2. Baking--Fiction. 3. Animals--Fiction.] I. Munsinger, Lynn, ill.
II. Title. III. Series.
PZ7.M1486He   1996
[E]--dc20   96-6346

This edition first published in 1996 by
Gareth Stevens Publishing
A World Almanac Education Group Company
330 West Olive Street, Suite 100
Milwaukee, Wisconsin 53212 USA

© 1990 by Byron Preiss Visual Publications, Inc. Text © 1990 by Maryann Macdonald.
Illustrations © 1990 by Lynn Munsinger.

Published by arrangement with Bantam Doubleday Dell Books for Young Readers,
a division of Bantam Doubleday Dell Publishing Group, Inc., New York, New York.
All rights reserved.

BANK STREET READY TO READ™ is a trademark of Bantam Doubleday Dell Books
For Young Readers, a division of Bantam Doubleday Dell Publishing Group, Inc.

All rights reserved. No part of this book may be reproduced, stored in a retrieval
system, or transmitted in any form or by any means, electronic, mechanical,
photocopying, or otherwise, without the prior written permission of the
copyright holder.

Printed in Mexico

4 5 6 7 8 9 05 04 03 02 01

Bank Street Ready-to-Read™

HEDGEHOG
Bakes a Cake

by Maryann Macdonald
Illustrated by Lynn Munsinger

A Byron Preiss Book

Gareth Stevens Publishing
A WORLD ALMANAC EDUCATION GROUP COMPANY

Hedgehog was hungry for cake.
He found a yellow cake recipe.
"This one sounds easy," he said,
"and good, too."

Hedgehog took out the flour.
He took out the eggs and the butter.

He was taking out the blue mixing bowl
when he heard a knock at the door.
It was Rabbit.
"Hello, Rabbit," said Hedgehog.
"I am making a cake."

"I will help you," said Rabbit.

"I am good at making cakes."

"Here is the recipe," said Hedgehog.

"You do not need this recipe," Rabbit said.

"I will show you what to do."

Rabbit took the flour.
He dumped it into the blue bowl.
He took the butter
and dumped that in, too.
Then he dumped in the sugar.
"Now we will mix it,"
said Rabbit.

Mixing was hard work.
Rabbit mixed and mixed.
His arm began to hurt.
The batter was lumpy.
The sugar stuck to the sides of the bowl.
There was flour everywhere.

"I think someone is calling me,"
said Rabbit.
"You finish the mixing, Hedgehog.
I will come back
when the cake is ready."

Hedgehog shook his head.
The cake batter was a mess.

"What's the matter, Hedgehog?"
Squirrel was at the door, looking in.
"I am making a cake," said Hedgehog.
"But it does not look very good."
"You need eggs," said Squirrel.
"I will put them in."

He cracked some eggs
and dropped them in.
Some shell fell in, too.
"A little bit of shell does not matter,"
said Squirrel.
"Mix it all together."
So Hedgehog mixed.
The batter was more lumpy,
but mixing was easier than before.

Owl stuck her head in the door.
"Baking?" she asked. "May I help?"
Hedgehog did not want more help.
But he didn't want to hurt Owl's feelings.

"You can butter the pan,"
said Hedgehog.
Owl was happy.
She stuck her wing into the butter.
Then she smeared it around the pan.

Owl turned on the oven
with her buttery feathers.
She turned it up as high as it would go.
"The oven must be nice and hot,"
she said.

"We have gotten very messy
helping you," said Squirrel.
"We will go home now and clean up.
Put the cake in the oven.
We will come back when it is ready."
Squirrel and Owl went home.

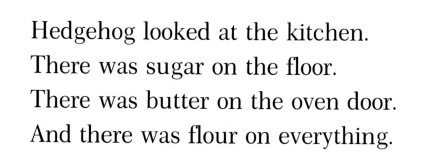

Hedgehog looked at the kitchen.
There was sugar on the floor.
There was butter on the oven door.
And there was flour on everything.

Hedgehog dumped the cake batter
into the garbage pail.
He locked the kitchen door
and took out his recipe.

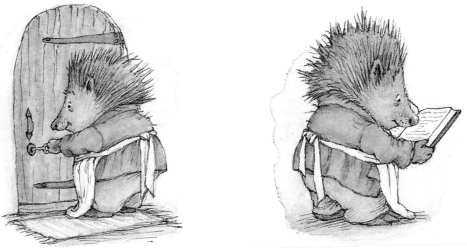

First Hedgehog measured the sugar.
He mixed it slowly with the butter.
Next he counted out three eggs
and cracked them into the bowl—
one, two, three.
Then he added the flour.

Hedgehog mixed everything together
and poured it into Owl's buttery pan.

SAGINAW CHIPPEWA ACADEMY
LIBRARY MEDIA CENTER
MT. PLEASANT, MI 48858

He turned down the heat
and put the batter in the oven.
Then he cleaned up the kitchen.

Knock, knock, knock.

"Open the door, Hedgehog,"
called Rabbit.

"We can smell the cake,
and we are getting hungry."

Hedgehog unlocked the door.

The kitchen was clean.

The cake was cooling on a rack.

And the table was set for a tea party.

The four friends sat down.
Hedgehog cut the cake.

They each ate one slice.
Then they each ate another slice.
"This is the best cake
I have ever made,"
said Rabbit.
"Aren't you glad I showed you
how to do it?"
"The eggs made it very rich,"
said Squirrel.
"And you can't taste the shell at all."

"It's perfect," said Owl.
"I set the oven just right."

"Thank you all for your help,"
said Hedgehog.
"Next time I will try to do it
all by myself."

HEDGEHOG'S YELLOW CAKE

1/2 cup (4 ounces) butter or margarine
1-1/4 cups (10 ounces) sugar
1-1/4 cups (5 ounces) sifted, all-purpose
   flour
2 eggs
1/2 cup (4 fluid ounces) milk
1 teaspoon vanilla extract
1 teaspoon baking soda
1/2 teaspoon salt

Ask an adult to set the oven to 350°
   Fahrenheit (175° Centigrade).
Then, butter a 9-inch (23-cm)-round pan.
Mix all the ingredients together in a bowl.

Pour batter into pan and bake for thirty
   to thirty-five minutes. Have an adult
   help you take the cake out of the oven
   when it is done.

Eat warm with a glass of milk.

Raised in a family of ten, Maryann Macdonald has spent most of her life with children. She graduated from the University of Michigan and has worked as a waitress, a truck driver, and a welfare worker. She has written several picture books and has recently published her first middle-grade novel, *Fatso Jean, the Ice Cream Queen.* Mrs. Macdonald lives in London, England, with her husband and two daughters.

Born in Greenfield, Massachusetts, Lynn Munsinger graduated from Tufts University and the Rhode Island School of Design. She has illustrated numerous books for children, including most recently *Ho For a Hat* and *One Hungry Monster,* as well as the much loved Hugh Pine books. Ms. Munsinger and her husband live in Winchester, Massachusetts, with their two dogs. When she's not working, she likes to read, ski, and travel.